POKÉMON ADVANCED

READER

POKÉMON IN DISGUISE!

Adapted by Tracey West

Scholastic Inc.

New York   Toronto   London   Auckland   Sydney

Mexico City   New Delhi   Hong Kong   Buenos Aires

ISBN 0-439-68672-5

12 11 10 9 8 7 6 5 4 3 2   4 5 6 7 8/0

Printed in the U.S.A.
First printing, November 2004

Ash and his friends were walking and talking about Pokémon.

"Being a trainer is all about making friends," Brock said.

"That is right," said Ash. "If you are not making friends, what is the point?"

Just then, a Zigzagoon ran by!
"Wow," Max said. "That is a really big
Zigzagoon!"

The Zigzagoon ran to a clearing. Many other Zigzagoon were there.

Then the big Zigzagoon took off its fur.

"That Zigzagoon is pretending to be a human," said Max's sister, May.

"No, silly. It is a human pretending to be a Zigzagoon," said Max.

Then Max called to the boy. "Hey, you! Who are you?"

"I have many names," said the boy.

He dressed like a Tentacruel.

"Tentacruel!"

He dressed like a Bellossom.

"Bellossom!"

"But my real name is Nicholai the Knicker Bocker," he said.

Nicholai pointed to his shorts. "I wear knickers to be closer to nature. You must be Knicker Bockers, too!"

"These are not knickers," said May. "They are just shorts!"

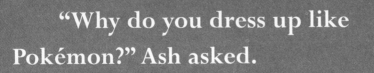

"Why do you dress up like Pokémon?" Ash asked.

"When I dress like a Pokémon, I feel like a Pokémon," said Nicholai. "It makes it easy to capture them."

"I want to capture a Zigzagoon," Nicholai said. "Then I want to challenge the leader of the Petalburg Gym."

Max beamed proudly. "The Petalburg Gym leader is our dad!" he said.

"He is?" Nicholai said. "Then I must battle one of you. It would be great practice."

"Show him what you can do, May," Max said.

May was nervous. She had never been in a Pokémon battle before.

"Okay," she said. "I will do it!"

Nicholai called on his Pokémon. "Mudkip, let's go!" he cried.

A little Water Pokémon popped out of his Poké Ball.

Then Nicholai got dressed up like a Mudkip!

May had to choose a Pokémon to battle Mudkip.

"Torchic, I choose you!" May yelled.

"Uh oh," said Max. "Torchic is a Fire Pokémon. It will not do well against a Water Pokémon."

The battle began.

"Torchic, use Ember!" May yelled.

"Mudkip, use Water Gun!" yelled
Nicholai.

Splash! Mudkip's water put out
Torchic's fire.

May tried another attack.

"Torchic, use Peck!" she yelled.

Torchic ran at Mudkip. But Mudkip used Water Gun again.

Wham! The attack made Torchic faint.

"Mudkip is the winner!" Brock said.

"Ha!" said Nicholai. "Beating you was easy. It will be easy to beat your dad, too." That made Max really angry!

Nicholai walked off. Ash and his friends went on their way.

Then May stopped. "Hey," she said. "Where is Max?"

Ash called on Taillow. "Go look for Max," he told the Flying Pokémon.

Max was following Nicholai.

"No one makes fun of my dad and gets away with it," Max said.

Max saw Nicholai throwing fruit to some Zigzagoon.

"He is trying to catch a Zigzagoon," Max said. "Maybe I can stop him!"

Max filled his shirt with fruit.

"Now all of the Zigzagoon will come to me," Max said.

The plan worked. The Zigzagoon came after Max.

"Uh oh!" Max said.

Taillow found Max just in time. Ash and Pikachu ran up.

Pikachu attacked the Zigzagoon with Thundershock.

"Pikachuuuuuu!"

The Zigzagoon ran away.

But the Zigzagoon came back. They looked angry.

"I think they want to eat!" May said.

Nicholai ran up in the nick of time. He
wore his Zigzagoon costume. He led the
angry Zigzagoon to a field of fruit trees.

"Mudkip, use Water Gun!" Nicholai yelled.

Mudkip shot water at the trees. The fruit fell off the branches. The hungry Zigzagoon began to munch on the fruit.

"Now I will catch a Zigzagoon," Nicholai said.

Splash! Mudkip used Water Gun to attack a Zigzagoon.

Whoosh! Nicholai threw out a Poké Ball.

"I caught a Zigzagoon!" Nicholai
cheered.

Then a metal claw came out of
nowhere. It grabbed Mudkip.

"Team Rocket!" Ash cried.

Jessie, James, and Meowth flew above them in a balloon.

"That Mudkip is ours now," said Jessie.

The metal claw lifted Mudkip into the balloon!

"Pikachuuuuu!" Pikachu tried to shock Team Rocket.

But a metal dish came out of the balloon.

The Electric Attack bounced off the metal dish.

"I am coming, Mudkip!" Nicholai cried.

He put on an Aipom costume. He climbed up a hill to get to the balloon.

Then he put on a Gligar costume. He glided to the balloon. He grabbed Mudkip!

"Taillow, use Peck to pop the balloon!" Ash yelled.

The balloon popped. Team Rocket fell to the ground—right into a hole dug by the Zigzagoon!

But Team Rocket would not give up without a battle. They called on Arbok and Weezing.

Boom! Pikachu zapped Arbok and Weezing. They slammed into Jessie, James, and Meowth.

"Looks like we are blasting off again!" they cried.

"Thank you for helping us," Max told Nicholai.

"I am glad we could help each other," Nicholai said. "That is what trainers do."

Then Nicholai challenged Ash to a battle. He used his Zigzagoon.

"I will use Taillow," said Ash. "It is Taillow's first battle, too."

"Cool," said Max. "They are both using new Pokémon. It is like they are having their first battle ever."

"I guess Pokémon trainers always have something to learn," said May. "Right, Pikachu?"

"Pika!" Pikachu agreed.